Margaret Hillert's

Why We Have Thanksgiving

A Beginning-to-Read Book

Illustrated by Stephen Marchesi

DEAR CAREGIVER,

The books in this Beginning-to-Read collection may look somewhat familiar in that the original versions could have been a part of your own early reading experiences. These carefully written texts feature common sight words to provide your child multiple exposures to the words appearing most frequently in written text. These new versions have been updated and the engaging illustrations are highly appealing to a contemporary audience of young readers.

Begin by reading the story to your child, followed by letting him or her read familiar words and soon your child will be able to read the story independently. At each step of the way, be sure to praise your reader's efforts to build his or her confidence as an independent reader. Discuss the pictures and encourage your child to make connections between the story and his or her own life. At the end of the story, you will find reading activities and a word list that will help your child practice and strengthen beginning reading skills. These activities, along with the comprehension questions are aligned to current standards, so reading efforts at home will directly support the instructional goals in the classroom.

Above all, the most important part of the reading experience is to have fun and enjoy it!

Shannon Cannon

Shannon Cannon,
Literacy Consultant

Norwood House Press • www.norwoodhousepress.com
Beginning-to-Read™ is a registered trademark of Norwood House Press.
Illustration and cover design copyright ©2017 by Norwood House Press. All Rights Reserved.

Authorized adapted reprint from the U.S. English language edition, entitled Why We Have Thanksgiving by Margaret Hillert. Copyright © 2017 Margaret Hillert. Reprinted with permission. All rights reserved. Pearson and Why We Have Thanksgiving are trademarks, in the US and/or other countries, of Pearson Education, Inc. or its affiliates. This publication is protected by copyright, and prior permission to re-use in any way in any format is required by both Norwood House Press and Pearson Education. This book is authorized in the United States for use in schools and public libraries.

Designer: Lindaanne Donohoe
Editorial Production: Lisa Walsh

LIBRARY OF CONGRESS CATALOGING-IN-PUBLICATION DATA

Names: Hillert, Margaret, author. I Marchesi, Stephen, illustrator.
Title: Why we have Thanksgiving / by Margaret Hillert ; illustrated by
  Stephen Marchesi.
Description: Chicago, IL : Norwood House Press, [2016] I Series: A
  beginning-to-read book I Summary: An easy-to-read fictional retelling of
  the journey of the Pilgrims to America, their struggles during the first
  year, and celebration of the first Thanksgiving. Includes reading
  activities and a word list. I Description based on print version record
  and CIP data provided by publisher; resource not viewed.
Identifiers: LCCN 2016020725 (print) I LCCN 2016001932 (ebook) I ISBN
  9781603579711 (eBook) I ISBN 9781599538099 (library edition : alk. paper)
Subjects: I CYAC: Thanksgiving Day--Fiction. I Pilgrims (New Plymouth
  Colony)--Fiction.
Classification: LCC PZ7.H558 (print) I LCC PZ7.H558 Whi 2016 (ebook) I DDC
  [E]--dc23
LC record available at https://lccn.loc.gov/2016020725

288N—072016
Manufactured in the United States of America in North Mankato, Minnesota.

I want you to go there.
You have to do what I want.
Go there. Go there.

We do not want to go there.
We do not like it.
We want to do what we like.

You can not do what you like.
Get in here.
Get in here.
This is the spot for you.

We do not like this.
Oh, we do not like this.
What can we do?
What can we do?

We can go away.
Yes, we can go away.
That is what we can do.
We can go in a boat.
A big, big boat.

Come on. Come on.
Get this on the boat.
We have to have it.
Work, work, work.

Oh, what a big boat!
We will go on it with
Mother and Father.
We will go away on it.

Here we are on the boat.
This is fun.
Away we go.

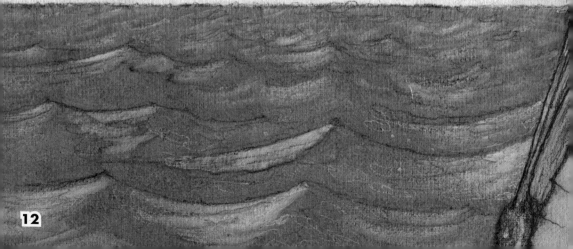

Away we go.
But where will we go?
What will we see?

Oh, look.
Do you see that?
Will we like it here?

Look up, up.
Look at that.
Do you see what I see?
How funny.

Come on.
Run, run, run.
This is fun for us.
Fun for you and me.

I guess Father and Mother
did not like it there.
Here we are on a boat.
Now where will we go?

What is this spot?
Is it a good one?
What will we do here?

We have to work.
We have to make a big
house for boys and girls
and mothers and fathers.

Oh, this is good.
Now Father can make
a house for us.
We can help.
See what we can do.

Look out. Look out.
Who is that?
What will he do?
Help! Help!

24

Why, he wants to help.
What a big help he is.
This is good.

See this come up,
and this,
and this.
It is good to eat.

And here is something
to eat, too.
Something little.
Something good.
We can get some for
Mother and Father.

Now, sit down. Sit down.
It is good to have
something to eat.
It is good to have friends.

Foundational Skills

In addition to reading the numerous high-frequency words in the text, this book also supports the development of foundational skills.

Phonological Awareness: The /w/ sound

Oral Blending: Say the beginning and ending sounds of the following words and ask your child to listen to the sounds and say the whole word:

/w/ + ill = will	/w/ + ing = wing	/w/ + all = wall
/w/ + eek = week	/w/ + ith = with	/w/ + ell = well
/w/ + ould = would	/w/ + alk – walk	/w/ + in = win
/w/ + ash = wash	/w/ + ide = wide	/w/ + ink = wink

Phonics: The letter Ww

1. Demonstrate how to form the letters **W** and **w** for your child.
2. Have your child practice writing **W** and **w** at least three times each.
3. Ask your child to point to the words in the book that begin with the letter **w**.
4. Write down the following words and ask your child to circle the letter **w** in each word:

how	water	wait	swing	flower
who	what	sew	when	sweep
now	work	swim	fewer	went

Fluency: Shared Reading

1. Reread the story to your child at least two more times while your child tracks the print by running a finger under the words as they are read. Ask your child to read the words he or she knows with you.
2. Reread the story taking turns, alternating readers between sentences or pages.

Language

The concepts, illustrations, and text help children develop language both explicitly and implicitly.

Vocabulary: Suffix -ful

1. Explain to your child that the suffix –ful means "full of".
2. Say the following words and ask your child to add the suffix –ful to each one:

   joy + ful = joyful   care + ful = careful   thank + ful = thankful
   help + ful = helpful   grate + ful = grateful   truth + ful = truthful
   respect + ful = respectful thought + ful = thoughtful   peace + ful = peaceful

3. Write each word on a separate piece of paper.
4. Read each word aloud for your child.
5. Take turns with your child pointing to a word and describing a time when you were…(…joyful, careful, thankful, etc.).

Reading Literature and Informational Text

To support comprehension, ask your child the following questions. The answers either come directly from the text or require inferences and discussion.

Key Ideas and Detail

- Ask your child to retell the sequence of events in the story.
- What happened to the people that did not obey the king?

Craft and Structure

- Is this a book that tells a story or one that gives information? How do you know?
- How do you think the children felt when they left their home?

Integration of Knowledge and Ideas

- Why do you think the man taught them how to grow corn?
- How does your family celebrate Thanksgiving?

WORD LIST

Why We Have Thanksgiving uses the 72 words listed

below. This list can be used to practice reading the words that appear in the text. You may wish to write the words on index cards and use them to help your child build automatic word recognition. Regular practice with these words will enhance your child's fluency in reading connected text.

a	Father(s)	I	oh	up
and	for	in	on	us
are	friends	is	one	
at	fun	it	out	want(s)
away	funny			we
		like	run	what
big	get	little		where
boat	girls	look	see	who
boys	go		sit	why
but	good		some	will
	guess	make	something	with
can		me	spot	work
come	have	Mother(s)		
	he		that	yes
did	help	not	the	you
do	here	now	there	
down	how		this	
	house		to	
eat			too	

ABOUT THE AUTHOR Margaret Hillert has helped millions of children all over the world learn to read independently. She was a first grade teacher for 34 years and during that time started writing books that her students could both gain confidence in reading and enjoy. She wrote well over 100 books for children just learning to read. As a child, she enjoyed writing poetry and continued her poetic writings as an adult for both children and adults.

Photograph by Glenna Washburn

ABOUT THE ILLUSTRATOR At an early age, Stephen Marchesi was creating and drawing super heroes for his own comic books. Inspired by adventure and monster movie posters of the nineteen-sixties, his love of classic illustration lead him to the works of 19th century masters. Stephen's paintings and drawings have appeared on over five hundred book covers for the young adult market, and he recently completed his fifty-first picture book.